THE TREASURE OF LI-PO

The Treasure Of
LI-PO

ALICE RITCHIE

With Illustrations by
T. RITCHIE

London
The Hogarth Press

PUBLISHED BY

The Hogarth Press Ltd

LONDON

o

Clarke, Irwin & Co Ltd

TORONTO

ISBN 0 7012 0305 6

First Published 1948
Reprinted 1968
Reprinted 1971

Printed in Great Britain by
Lewis Reprints Limited, Port Talbot
Glamorgan

Contents

* ❧ *

Illustrations

The Treasure of Li-Po

The Treasure of Li-Po

* 🐛 *

L I-PO, the basket-maker, lived all alone on the banks
of the Yang-tse river, far away from towns and the
busy world. In fact, he was some distance even
from the nearest village, and he hardly ever went into it,
but every morning and every evening he looked towards
it, and seeing the smoke from the cooking-stoves and the
little lights in the houses, he would say: 'Well, we are
both getting old, and neither of us is very big or very
rich, but we are managing to hold our own, I think. We
are not doing too badly.' And then he would rub his
hands together and chuckle, for he was a simple old man,
and kind and good, and although he did not see anyone
from the village for months at a time, he wished them
all well.

Twice a year, a merchant came from a far-off city to
buy the baskets he made from the bamboos on the banks
of the river. He stayed one night with Li-Po in his hut
and his servants slept in tents around it. So poor and
small was the hut that you might say for that night the
servants were housed better than their master, but the
merchant was fond of Li-Po, and thought his conversa-
tion and his kindness made up for the very simple entertainment which was all he could offer. In the morning
he paid him and loaded the baskets on to his travelling

Every evening he looked towards the village

wagon and off they all went, leaving the old man alone again for another six months.

Now it happened one·day shortly before the merchant was due to arrive, that a notion came into Li-Po's head to count his money. He kept it in a sack under his bed and each time the merchant paid him he pushed the new coins in along with the old ones and thought no more about them, for he had little need of money. He grew his own vegetables and caught fish in the river and pumped his drink from the well in the courtyard. Living that quiet life, one coat lasted him for a long time. What did he want with money? But he had been making baskets for fifty years, and even small pay mounts up in that time; when he began to pull out the sack, it was so heavy he could hardly move it.

'Here's a business,' he said to himself, 'there's a terrible weight here.'

At last he got it out, and then he found that the sack had lain there for so long that the rats had nibbled a large hole in it, and he had to go creeping under the bed to gather up the stray coins.

'Sharp teeth,' he said, 'but not sharp wits, for what good is money to a rat? And, for that matter,' he added, as he counted it, 'what good is money to me?'

He was quite dismayed when he found how much there was, and he sat for a while beside the pile on the floor wondering what to do. But after some time he had an idea which pleased him very much, and he chuckled to himself as he found a new sack and tied the money up securely and then went out to look for the approach of the merchant.

Presently a cloud of dust appeared on the horizon, and soon he saw the wagon and could make out the figure of his friend riding ahead of it. Then all was bustle in his quiet home—buckets of water drawn from the well for the thirsty beasts; rice cakes and a freshly cooked fish set out for the merchant, an old fan taken down from the wall for him to refresh himself with after the dusty ride, and Li-Po standing on the edge of his little property to greet him.

When the meal was eaten the merchant asked Li-Po to share with him a bottle of the wine he always carried on his journeys, and they went out on to the verandah and filled their cups and drank and watched the sun set over the river. The water-lilies were closing for the night; nothing moved except a long-legged heron which walked slowly down to the river bank and then stood like a statue, watching for fish.

'It is very peaceful here,' said the merchant. 'In some ways I envy your lot.'

'Yes, it is peaceful,' said Li-Po, who had never lived anywhere else, 'but I have something on my mind and I want to ask your advice, as a man who has seen much of the world.'

'Now what can you possibly have to worry you?' asked the merchant, smiling to himself under his long moustache, 'for I will gladly help you in any way I can.'

'It is a question of money,' said Li-Po.

The merchant was so surprised at hearing the old man say he had some trouble connected with money that he found nothing to say, and Li-Po was always very slow in his thoughts and his speech, so they sat in silence for some time. The merchant lit his pipe and watched the sunset, and at last Li-Po spoke again.

'I should like you to tell me,' he said, 'the name of the most virtuous and accomplished young lady you have met in your travels.'

'That is easy,' said the merchant, although he did not see what this could have to do with Li-Po's troubles. 'Of all the ladies I have met the most virtuous and accomplished is undoubtedly Miss Ch'en Hua. She lives in the town of Honan, in the house of her father, and her heart is entirely inclined towards goodness. Her embroidery work is the admiration of all her acquaintance, and she plays upon the lute in the most ravishing manner. In addition to this she is so beautiful that a large crowd is always standing at her father's gates in the hope that their eyes will be rewarded by simply seeing her go in or out.'

'Good, good,' said Li-Po, grunting and chuckling. 'Now, my friend, I have a favour to ask of you. It happens that I have a great deal of money which I do not want. Will you take it when you go away tomorrow, and buy a jewel with it, and give it to Miss Ch'en Hua with the good wishes of one who admires virtue far more than he cares for money.'

'Certainly I will,' said the merchant, 'but allow me to say that I am surprised to hear you have so much money to spare, and I wonder whether it would not be wiser for you to keep it in case you are ever ill or in need.'

'No,' said Li-Po, 'for myself, I shall trust, as I have always trusted, in Providence. But money lying in my house gives me a heavy feeling about the heart. It is not suitable for me to be rich.'

'Very well,' said the merchant, 'I shall do as you ask.'

And the next morning when the wagon set out again he took Li-Po's sack of money with him, carefully strapped on his own saddle.

Li-Po had begged him to take a share of it as payment for his trouble, but he was a rich man, and besides he was too fond of Li-Po to count a service done for him as tiresome, so he spent every coin in the sack on a little necklace of carved green jade. He took it with him the next time he visited the town of Honan, and went straight to the house of Miss Ch'en Hua's father.

'You must have an interesting life,' said the father, as they sat drinking tea. 'You see a great deal of the world.'

'I see some strange things,' said the merchant. He smiled at Miss Ch'en Hua, who sat beside her father, and took the necklace out of his wallet and handed it to her. 'What, for instance, do you say to this? I have been asked to give it to you with the good wishes of someone who lives far from here and who has never seen you, but who admires virtue far more than he cares for money.'

'Oh, oh,' said Miss Ch'en Hua, covering her face with her hands, for she was as modest as she was beautiful.

'Well, really,' said her father, taking the necklace out of her lap to examine it, 'it is a fine piece of work. The giver must be a man of taste.'

The merchant did not say he had chosen it himself, because he wanted Li-Po to have all the credit for the gift. Presently he was pleased to see Miss Ch'en Hua fasten it round her neck.

'Oh, oh,' said Miss Ch'en Hua

When his visit was over and he was standing in the courtyard waiting for his horse to be brought for him, Miss Ch'en Hua came out of the house carrying a packet.

'Please give this small present to the person who sent the jade necklace,' she said, 'and say that it comes from one who admires a generous heart far more than she cares for jewels,' then, pressing the packet into the merchant's hands and veiling her blushes with her fan, she went quickly into the house.

'Now this is getting rather complicated,' said the merchant to himself, 'I very much doubt whether my old friend Li-Po will know what to do with a present from Miss Ch'en Hua.'

However, he was anxious to deliver it, and one day a little later when his business took him near to where Li-Po lived, he rode over to the old man's hut.

When Li-Po saw him coming he ran to meet him, surprised at seeing him again so soon.

'I have not made enough baskets yet for it to be worth your while to come,' he said.

'It is not baskets which bring me here,' said the merchant, 'I have been entrusted with a present for you.'

'A present,' said Li-Po, in dismay, 'who would send me a present?'

'Miss Ch'en Hua, to whom I gave a carved jade necklace from you, sends you this with good wishes from one who admires a generous heart far more than she loves jewels,' said the merchant, handing the packet to Li-Po.

Li-Po found the silken strings difficult to untie, because his hands were roughened with hard work, but at last he managed it, and the wrappings fell off and they saw a most beautiful scarf-band embroidered all over in silk of every colour with little figures of noble youths at play.

'It is the work of her own hands,' said the merchant. 'No one is her equal for embroidery.'

'Alas,' said Li-Po, touching the silk gently for fear of spoiling it, 'this is a present fit for a gallant prince. I should be ashamed to have such a beautiful thing. Tell me,' he said, 'the name of the most generous and noble young man you have met in your travels.'

'That is easy,' said the merchant. 'Of all the youths I have met the most generous and noble is undoubtedly the young lord Yuan-Sen. He lives in the town of Yunan, and the people who are under his rule are the happiest in the world.'

'Good, good,' said Li-Po. 'Then, my friend, I beg you will take this scarf-band to him with the good wishes of one who admires a generous heart.'

'Very well,' said the merchant, thinking that after all it was a pity the beautiful embroidery should not be used, 'I shall take it to him.'

And, sure enough, soon after, he went to the province of Yunan and took Miss Ch'en Hua's packet and gave it to the young lord Yuan-Sen with 'the good wishes of one who admires a generous heart'.

'This is very strange,' said Yuan-Sen, unfolding the packet, 'I do not understand why I should be given such a present——' for he was as modest as he was noble. When he unwrapped the packet and saw the embroidered scarf-band, he blushed and said. 'This is the gift of a lady, and she must have the most beautiful fingers in the world, for never have I seen its equal.'

Now the merchant did not like to say that it was really the gift of a poor old man who wore the same blue coat year after year and whose fingers were rough and coarse with basket-making, so he smiled and said nothing.

But Yuan-Sen was not willing to let matters rest at that, and when the merchant was leaving he sent for him and showed him an enormous collection of parcels and packages each stamped with his own mark, a crescent moon and a phoenix.

'I wish you to take these as an offering to the giver of the scarf-band,' he said, 'and say they come with the good wishes of one who admires the skill of hands more than all the treasures in his province.'

'I shall have to get an extra horse to carry that load,' said the merchant.

'I shall give you a horse for your trouble,' said the lordly Yuan-Sen, and a fine horse was led up and all the parcels were loaded on to it and securely tied.

The merchant rode at once with the treasures to Li-Po on the banks of the Yang-tse river.

The old man was surprised to see him coming and when he heard his story he wrung his hands in despair.

'Let us see what he has sent you, at all events,' said the merchant. He untied one of the parcels, and then even he, who had seen so much of the world, fell back with a loud exclamation of surprise, and as for Li-Po, he covered his eyes with his hands as if he was not fit even to look at the treasures it contained—gold and silver drinking cups, birds and fishes carved out of precious

'It is not mine!' cried Li-Po

stones, painted ivory screens, they lay in a heap at their feet on the mud floor of Li-Po's hut.

'It is not mine, it is not mine!' cried Li-Po.

'It is yours,' said the merchant, 'the lord Yuan-Sen gave it with the good wishes of one who admires the skill of hands more than all the treasures in his province. And no one can deny,' he added slyly, 'that you have great skill in your hands and much practice in using it for fifty years in making baskets. Li-Po, you are now a very rich man.'

He bent down to undo another parcel, but Li-Po stopped him.

'No, no,' he said, 'leave the rest. Let us tie this one up again, and then, my friend, I beg you to take it all away and give it to Miss Ch'en Hua with the same message as the lord Yuan-Sen sent to me. But please take something out of it to repay you for your trouble.'

'Very well,' said the merchant, 'I will do as you say, but I am afraid this business is going to have a bad ending. And, as I shall have to neglect my other work to go to the town of Honan, I shall take this silver cup to repay me for my time, though you know I am always glad to serve you.'

Li-Po thanked him and they tied up the parcel of treasures again and the merchant set off for the town of Honan.

As soon as he got there he went straight to the house of Miss Ch'en Hua's father and led the horse loaded with presents into the courtyard. Then he called to Miss Ch'en Hua to come and see what he had brought.

'You have a great load of merchandise there,' said

Miss Ch'en Hua's father, coming into the courtyard with his daughter. 'Where are you going to sell it?'

'I am not going to sell it,' said the merchant. 'It is for Miss Ch'en Hua, with the good wishes of one who admires the skill of hands more than all the treasures in his province.'

Without thinking, he had given the whole of Yuan-Sen's message, and as soon as he said it he bit his lip, so that he should not smile when he remembered that all the treasures which Li-Po owned in *his* province were the sun and the wind and the water-lilies on the Yang-tse river, and when Miss Ch'en Hua's father said, 'which is the province of the giver of this princely gift?' he answered, still with his mind full of Li-Po, 'the Yang-tse province.' Miss Ch'en Hua and her father were amazed at the magnificent present, and when the parcels and packets were unwrapped they were so overcome that for some time they could not speak.

'Now I have done my duty, and I must go,' said the merchant, who was beginning to feel uneasy about the whole business; but Miss Ch'en Hua's father put his hand on his arm and held him back.

'Not so fast,' he said, 'not so fast. I see now what all this means.' He turned to his daughter who was still staring as if she was in a dream at the gold and silver and jade and ivory and precious silks which filled the whole courtyard. 'It is quite clear that this present comes from a great lord,' he said. 'See, here is his emblem on the wrappings—a crescent moon and a phoenix—no one but a great lord would have such an emblem, and it is quite clear too that he wishes to marry you. Really, I think, my dear child, that you could not do better. What do you say?'

Miss Ch'en Hua answered in a trembling voice that she would like to see the giver of the present before anything was decided.

'Very well,' said her father, 'we shall pay a visit to this princely young man in the Yang-tse province. You must guide us to his palace,' he said to the merchant, who trembled in his shoes and wished he had never had anything to do with Li-Po or Yuan-Sen or Miss Ch'en Hua. 'We shall start in a month from this day; that will give me time to prepare, for we must go in State and we must take some rich offerings. Do not forget,' he said, fixing the merchant sternly with his eye, rather annoyed with him for not showing more interest in the scheme, 'in a month from this day you must be in the courtyard to guide us, and mind, if you do not come, I shall ruin your trade in this town and in the eight towns round about it.'

'Oh father,' cried Miss Ch'en Hua, 'do not speak so harshly to our kind friend who has brought this honour to me,' and she bent down and gathered up gold and silver ornaments and pressed them on the merchant until his arms were full.

He blessed her and packed them on his horse, but do what he would, he could not speak with enthusiasm about the expedition to the Yang-tse river. His heart sank when he thought of Li-Po's poor hut, with nothing in it but an old bed and one old table, and the rice cakes and the fish and the well-water which were the most he could provide for his guests. He did not know what was to be done. However, Miss Ch'en Hua's father was a powerful man, so he had to promise that in a month's time he would be in the courtyard and would guide them to the home of the unknown giver of presents in the Yang-tse province.

Then, as he was turning away, wondering how he could break the news to Li-Po, Miss Ch'en Hua came up to him while her father was busy watching the servants carry the treasure into the house. She gave him a parcel and said: 'Please give it to the one who sent me the present and say I hope he will wear it at our meeting,' and although the merchant had had more than enough of this business of presents, he could not refuse Miss Ch'en Hua, because she looked so beautiful, blushing and smiling and bowing in front of him. So he took the parcel and turned his horse's head and rode as fast as he could, day and night, to Li-Po in the Yang-tse province.

The old man came out to meet him; this time he guessed that the visit must have something to do with the presents and his face was full of anxiety before the merchant had even alighted from his horse.

'We are ruined,' said the merchant, 'Miss Ch'en Hua's father is a proud man, and powerful. He will never forgive me if I do not bring him here, and when he comes, what will you do?'

Li-Po wrung his hands. 'Alas,' he said, 'I am thinking of the beautiful and accomplished Miss Ch'en Hua. When she finds an old man in a poor hut at the end of her journey she will think a cruel trick has been played on her. There is only one thing I can do, my friend, to spare her this shame. I must die.'

'Do not speak like that,' said the merchant. 'We must think of a plan.' But he could not think of anything.

'She sent you this,' he said at last, giving Li-Po Miss Ch'en Hua's parcel, 'and I was to say that she hoped the giver of the presents would wear it at the meeting.'

With trembling hands Li-Po untied the silken strings and unwrapped an embroidered silk coat suitable for a nobleman to wear in the flower of his youth. He groaned and his tears ran down.

'Now we see how cruelly she has been deceived,' he said, 'she will die of shame when she comes here. But take it to the young lord Yuan-Sen, so at least it will have a worthy owner. And then if no plan occurs to you, you must keep your word and go back to meet Miss Ch'en Hua's father.'

'But what will you do?' asked the merchant. 'Promise me that you will think no more of dying.'

Li-Po shook his head. 'I am a foolish old man,' he said, 'I should have died long ago before I brought shame upon the beautiful and virtuous Miss Ch'en Hua.' And as that was all he would say, the merchant left him and took the coat to the young lord Yuan-Sen. But he had not the heart to make up a message, and when Yuan-Sen began to exclaim about the lovely coat and to ask questions about its maker, he told him the whole story about Li-Po and the sack of money, and how one thing had led to another until at last the old man was sitting in his little hut grieving and wishing he might die.

'So the one thing I must not do is to send a gift of any kind,' said Yuan-Sen smiling. 'You and he have both had enough to do with gifts.'

'You had better give her this ring'

'That is true,' said the merchant.

'And yet it will look strange if you go back to meet Miss Ch'en Hua and to guide her to the Yang-tse province and take no offering in your hand. You had better give her this ring.' And he handed the merchant a gold ring set with an emerald as big as a pigeon's egg.

The merchant took the ring, though he did not see that it mattered much whether he brought a present or not, when the end of the journey was bound to be so disappointing.

'My advice to you,' went on Yuan-Sen, 'is to say nothing to the father or to Miss Ch'en Hua, but simply to bring them to where the old man lives. Who knows? God may help the simple-hearted in a way you cannot guess.'

So the merchant rode off, and as he had not thought of any plan, he did not go back to Li-Po but went straight to Honan to meet Miss Ch'en Hua and her father.

Li-Po sat on the banks of the Yang-tse river, too unhappy to do his basket work, and too poor to make any preparations for his guests. Each day as he watched the sun set, he thought: 'Now we are one day nearer to the meeting. If I do not die before then, I shall die of shame on that morning.' And he forgot to look towards the village with his blessing, and could not take pleasure in the water-lilies or the herons or any of the things which used to please him.

At last, one day, when he looked up from his sad brooding, he saw a huge cloud of dust on the horizon and soon he made out the shapes of many men on horseback and a great number of wagons. 'Alas, alas,' he cried, running to and fro in his grief, 'they are coming a full day before their time, and here am I, still alive!' He went into his hut and sat with his head bowed on his hands. He tried not to hear the sound of the arrival of the horses and wagons, though the air was full of the merry shouts of the riders and drivers. He buried his head in his arms and tried not to hear or to see. Then someone came into the hut and he felt a hand on his shoulder, and thinking it must be his friend the merchant, he looked up with a groan. A young man of the handsomest and noblest appearance was standing there smiling at him.

'What can you want with me?' asked Li-Po.

'I want you to adopt me,' said the young man, still smiling and still keeping his hand on Li-Po's shoulder.

'Alas, it is a sad thing that so gallant a young man must be mad,' said Li-Po.

The young man laughed. 'I am not mad,' he said; 'Li-Po, I am the lord Yuan-Sen and I know all about your trouble and have come to deliver you from it. Listen, you must adopt me as your nephew, and then when Miss Ch'en Hua and her father come I shall wear the coat and scarf she sent and you will say you gave them to me because they were more suitable for a young man than an old one.'

'Still that will not save her,' said Li-Po, 'what will she think when she finds herself in this poor hut?'

'Come outside and you shall see something,' said the young man, smiling more broadly than ever, 'But first tell me,' he went on, shaking Li-Po's shoulder a little, 'will you have me for a nephew?'

'I should be proud to have such a fine youth for my nephew,' said Li-Po, with a faint hope arising in his heart, and they embraced as relations do.

Then they went outside the hut together and Li-Po gasped with surprise. All the men whom Yuan-Sen had brought with him were busily at work building the most magnificent pavilion out of materials they had brought with them in the wagons. Some of them were clearing the ground for the polished floors to rest on, others were unpacking the red lacquer which was to make the walls. They had already set up a peal of golden bells where the entrance was to be, and were unloading chests containing rich carpets and silks and fine silver drinking cups and china plates and big gold dishes, and crates of rare and delicate food and precious wine.

'We shall not lack for anything in our entertainment, uncle,' said Yuan-Sen. 'Before sunset everything will be in place, and tomorrow morning you must put on this gold robe and this crimson cap to do honour to your guests.'

'Nay,' said Li-Po, 'I think, nephew, I had better put it on now, for I shall need some practice in wearing a golden robe and a crimson cap.'

The next morning the carriages and horses of Miss Ch'en Hua's father were drawing near to the place where Li-Po had his hut. The merchant rode a little ahead of them, because he was so anxious and unhappy; he was not only afraid of the revenge Miss Ch'en Hua's father would take on him when he found a poor old man instead of a rich young one, but also he was afraid that Li-Po might no longer be alive. So he looked eagerly for the first sight of the little hut, as if that in itself could tell him something. He looked, and then rubbed his eyes and looked again. He thought his mind must be giving way, or that he had missed the road, although he knew it as well as the road to his own house, for there, a few hundred yards away, stood a rose-coloured pavilion with green lattice verandahs and a gilt roof, and even at this distance he could hear the sweet peal of golden bells ringing in welcome.

Miss Ch'en Hua's father rode up and joined him. 'It is a fine looking house,' he said.

'It is indeed,' said the merchant, staring, and wishing he could gallop quickly in advance of the others to find out what mysterious thing had happened.

'I think I can see our host at the gate,' said Miss Ch'en Hua's father, and the merchant narrowed his eyes and looked, and sure enough, there stood his old friend Li-Po dressed in a gorgeous robe which glittered in the morning sunlight, and a crimson cap on his head. The merchant nearly fell off his horse with surprise and joy. Then he saw another person come out of the pavilion and stand beside Li-Po. He wore the embroidered coat Miss Ch'en Hua had sent, and the merchant soon recognized him to be the lordly and gallant Yuan-Sen. It was all he could do not to throw up his cap and shout, for now he understood everything and it was as perfect as the best dream he had ever had in his life.

They woke Miss Ch'en Hua, who had been sleeping in her carriage, and she smoothed her lovely hair and put on the emerald ring the merchant had brought for her, and then they rode up to the gate and Li-Po ran forward

to greet them with Yuan-Sen at his side, and they all
went into the pavilion to the gay sound of the bells and
of many stringed instruments.

It was love at first sight with the young lord Yuan-Sen
and Miss Ch'en Hua. Her father gladly gave his consent
to their marriage, Li-Po gave his as gladly, and no one
took a livelier part in the rejoicings at the wedding than
the merchant.

At last the time came for the father to go home again
and for the two young people to leave for Yuan-Sen's
province. They took tender farewells of Li-Po, and
Yuan-Sen, leading him a little apart from the rest, said:
'Uncle, I wish to leave a number of servants behind to
look after you in the red pavilion, and also enough money
for you to be comfortable there.'

'I beg you to do nothing of the kind,' said Li-Po.
'Your society and the society of Miss Ch'en Hua, now
your wife, has been very pleasant to me, but once you
have gone I wish to go back to my old style of living.
Believe me, nephew, there was never a more con-
tented man than I was in my hut. I should not know what
to do with either servants or money. In fact, I ask you
as a last favour to bid some of your servants stay behind
to remove the red pavilion, for I should not enjoy it
alone.'

'I must do as you say, Uncle,' said Yuan-Sen, 'but I
wish I might have had my way. Once a year I shall come
to visit you, and the hut which shelters you will always
be fine enough for me.'

They embraced with great affection, as relations do.
Then Yuan-Sen joined his bride and they set off for the

It was love at first sight

province of Yunan, and the father went back to Honan, and the merchant rode away somewhere on his business. But before *he* left Li-Po said, 'I shall expect to see you in six months' time, as usual.'

'I shall be glad to come,' said the merchant, 'but what use will you have for my services now?'

'Why, to sell my baskets, of course!' said Li-Po, staring at him in surprise.

The servants whom Yuan-Sen left behind made haste to pull down and pack up the red lacquer pavilion and the silks and carpets and fine china. Soon they loaded it up on wagons and then they too were gone.

But the young lord Yuan-Sen had not been able after all to leave Li-Po as poor as he had found him. 'I cannot bear it,' he said to himself, 'though I am afraid he will not be pleased.' And so he had hidden a sack of money under Li-Po's bed.

When the old man found it, he thought at first it was his old sack of coins, come back again by magic, but when he opened it and saw that they were gold this time instead of copper, he guessed who had put it there and he shook his head and grunted, but in the end he smiled.

'My nephew is very clever,' he said, 'but I am cleverer still. Last time I spent my money far afield. This time I shall spend it nearer home.' And he loaded the sack on to his old wheelbarrow and trundled it over to the village which he used to look at in the morning and the evening. He called to the headman to come out and he gave him the sack of coins to spend on the poor people, 'so that no one shall ever be cold and hungry in this village again,' he said.

The headman of the village was a good man and he rejoiced. 'It is a small village,' he said, 'but there was suffering in the cold weather last year; with this enormous sum of money that need never happen again. We wondered some time ago to see a red lacquer palace go up beside your hut,' he added with a shy smile, 'but now it has gone again.'

'Yes,' said Li-Po, also smiling shyly, 'now it has gone again. I must go home because I have lost a good deal of time lately and I am behind in my basket work.'

But Li-Po's name was blessed ever after by all the people in that village, and Yuan-Sen and his wife loved him to the end of his days.

The
Faithful Lantern-Bearer

The
Faithful Lantern-Bearer

* 🐉 *

THE Lord of the country of Han, which we now
call China, was going on a journey. He set out
from the Eastern Gate in the early morning, and
all his councillors and courtiers followed him. They
looked at the frost which covered the grass and they
shivered until their jade neck-chains rattled. The wind
struck them between the shoulders as they sat on their
horses, and they muttered in their beards: 'now we see
that it is better to serve an old master than a young one,
for an old man lies in bed on the cold mornings, but a
young man is as restless as the chilly streams which we
shall soon be crossing.' They blew on their frozen hands
and shook the icicles from their beards. But the Lord of
Han galloped straight ahead over the plain towards the
mountains; what the courtiers were thinking did not
matter to him.

The courtiers and the councillors rode on horses, but
the lantern-bearers had to run on foot beside them,
holding on to their stirrups. Their lanterns were not lit
now, because the sun had risen. They pushed the long
sticks through their sashes so that their hands were free,
and their lanterns bobbed over their shoulders as they
ran. Wherever the Lord of Han went, these young boys

Here he dismounted

had to go too, because they were his closest bodyguard. They were chosen from the noblest families in the land of Han, and their boast was: 'Never parted from Lord or Lantern'. So they ran with swift feet and stout hearts over the plain.

At last, when they had all gone a great distance, the Lord of Han drew rein, and the councillors and courtiers at once pulled up their horses, and formed in a big semicircle to hear his orders. The Lord turned round and faced them; the sun shone on his embroidered sleeves and on the jewels in the dagger which he wore in his belt, and on his majestic head.

'Let only the lantern-bearers follow me now,' he said. 'The rest of you are to go back to the Palace. You will see me again when it pleases me to return.'

Well, the councillors and courtiers had grumbled when they set out in the frosty morning, but they had not disliked that so much as they disliked being dismissed in high noon-day from following their Lord on his journey, because all their glory was only a reflection of his, and when they were not with him they had nothing to do, and nothing to think about. But of course they could not say anything. They had to bow their heads and salute and wheel their horses about and set off at a gallop for the Palace.

The Lord of Han rode on towards the mountains at the edge of the great plain. He went more slowly now, and the lantern-bearers trotted behind him with their lanterns bob-bob-bobbing on their backs, until they came to the low hills covered with scrubby bushes where the plain ended and the mountains began. Here he dismounted and gave his horse to one of the lantern-bearers to hold. He walked away from them without saying anything, but when they began to follow him, he stopped and said: 'Wait for me here. You will see me again when it pleases me to return.' It was a terrible thing for them to see their Lord going alone towards the mountains on foot, and as they dared not speak, they all went down on their knees to show him their distress. He turned again and shook his head. 'Che'n Chu, the Hermit of the mountains, will not speak to anyone unless he comes unattended and on foot. Even for the Lord of Han he has no other rule.' Then they knew that he was going to visit the holy Hermit of the mountains, to drink a cup of wine with him and to talk about the highest matters, and that there was nothing for them to do but wait until he came back.

The sun was setting; its last light shone on his embroideries and jewels which had more colours in them than there are in a peacock's tail, and then he disappeared from their sight behind the great boulders on the mountain side.

'The light goes when the Lord goes,' said one of the lantern-bearers.

'We must light our lanterns,' said another.

'I must tether the horse,' said Lee-Su, the one to whom the Lord had handed his reins.

They lit their lanterns and drove the long sticks into the sandy ground and sat down to wait. Some of them repeated poetry to themselves, one played with dice, throwing left hand against right; the youngest went to sleep. But it grew colder, and presently he woke up

44

and felt for the rug which, of course, was not there. They began to be hungry too, for they had eaten nothing all day. Lee-Su found some scraps of rice bread in the wallet which he wore strapped round his middle, but he fed the horse with them, because, he said, 'He is even more necessary to our master than we are.'

It was now quite dark, and they could see nothing clearly outside the circle of their lanterns; the mountains were humps of blackness, and the plain was a sea of blackness.

'This is dragon country,' said one.

'I, too, have always been told that there are many dragons in this part,' said another, and they began to talk about the best way of catching dragons, or scaring them off, and some of them said that they rather wished a dragon would appear, so that they could test their method, which was to strike him sharply over the nose with a lighted lantern.

But Lee-Su said, 'For my part, I hope we shall not see one, because it would frighten the horse.'

As he said these words, the horse began to whinny and whimper and stamp its hooves. He got up and took his lantern and went over to it and put his hand on its neck.

'You are the noblest horse in the whole of the land of Han,' he said. 'Think how you are honoured above all other horses. Your shoes are made of gold, and your mane is plaited with ribbons and you carry the Lord of Han on your back. Please be comforted by thinking of these things.'

But the horse went on shivering and staring with wild eyes into the darkness, and now they heard a roaring sound and saw a red light in the distance, moving towards them over the plain. The other lantern-bearers sprang up and snatched their lanterns. The noise grew louder and the light grew brighter and they smelt sulphur in the air. The ground shook under their feet. Lee-Su put both his arms round the horse's neck. He thought to himself: 'The command the Lord gave us was to wait here. I do not know how to slay a dragon; it is better to die obeying orders than to die disobeying them,' and he laid his forehead against the horse's neck and shut his eyes. Soon, however, it seemed to him that the noise was less loud, and the smell of sulphur less strong; the horse ceased to shiver, and when Lee-Su opened his eyes there was not a sign of the red light.

But he was all alone. The other lantern-bearers had disappeared, taking their lanterns with them, and whether they had run towards the dragon to kill it, or away from it for fear it killed them, he did not know, because he had not had his eyes open to see.

He planted the stick of his lantern in the ground again and sat down beside it. The horse went peacefully to sleep. It was very dark and very quiet and very cold. He looked up at the stars and tried to pass the time by making them into shapes of men and dragons and horses. Suddenly he heard a little scratching noise near his foot, and looking down he saw a mouse, one of the long-tailed, long-nosed, fringy-eared kind that live among the Sesura bushes which grow on the edge of mountain country.

'Cree, cree, cree,' said the mouse, looking up at him with its bright eyes, 'What are you doing here?'

'I am waiting for my master,' said Lee-Su politely.

'Indeed!' said the mouse, 'Well, I suppose your master is a man like any other.'

'No,' said Lee-Su. 'There is no other man like my master. He is the Lord of Han.' He went on, 'this ground we are sitting on belongs to him, because it is part of the country of Han, and everything in the country of Han, or on it, or under it belongs to him; Mouse, you belong to him, and it is by his mercy that you live.'

'I pay no tribute to him,' said the mouse in an off-hand way, 'or to anybody else.'

'The Lord of Han does not need to take tribute from his mice,' said Lee-Su, 'he is the richest man in the world. But for all that you belong to him.'

'Does the dragon belong to him?' asked the mouse, curling its tail round its front feet.

'Certainly,' said Lee-Su.

'Oh, well,' said the mouse, shrugging its shoulders as if the subject did not much interest it.

'Where has the dragon gone?' asked Lee-Su.

'Home,' said the mouse, 'he usually takes a stroll before turning in for the night, but he doesn't care to be out late. He is not so young as he was.'

'Aren't you afraid of him?'

'I?' said the mouse, 'Oh, no, I am too small; he doesn't worry me. You see what a good thing it is to be small—I escape both the Lord of Han and the dragon.'

'That is not a correct way to speak,' said Lee-Su stiffly, and they sat in silence for a while. Lee-Su was so cold that he could hardly keep his teeth from chattering, but he made a great effort not to show anything in front of the mouse, for fear it said that there was

47

another good reason for being small—even quite poor people can afford a fur coat, if they are only three inches long.

It was picking its teeth with a straw, to show that it did not mind about not being talked to, when a long-legged bird, a Sesura heron with a grey body and a black head, came up and joined them.

'Human company is rare here at any time,' it said in a reedy voice, 'and I never remember seeing a human at night before. You must be very cold, surely, lacking both fur and feathers?'

'Not at all,' said Lee-Su, looking up at the stars and trying not to shiver.

'I have been watching you for some time,' said the heron, 'and wondering if you would like me to show you a place where you could have some shelter. Not very far from here, there is a hut which was built by a man who has since gone away. I don't suppose it is at all what you have been used to, but there is some straw in it which would keep you warm and comfortable till morning.'

'Where is this hut?' asked Lee-Su in an anxious voice.

'I should think it would take you, allowing for human slowness, if you will excuse my mentioning it, about half an hour to reach it. What do you say?'

But Lee-Su shook his head. 'It is too far,' he said. 'My orders were to wait here, and a place which is half an hour's distance from here is not *here*, so I should be disobeying orders if I went. Besides,' he added, 'I am not at all cold.'

It was picking its teeth with a straw

The heron and the mouse looked at each other.

'He has been telling me how great his master is,' said the mouse, in a more civil voice than before, 'he serves the Lord of Han. It is a great honour, but it seems to me that it sometimes puts him in very uncomfortable positions. His companions ran away some time ago when the old dragon came past.'

'They ran,' said Lee-Su, 'but it is not correct to say that they ran away. They may have been ——'

'I saw them,' interrupted the mouse, 'not that I blame them.'

'Well, well,' said the heron peaceably, standing on one leg and gathering the other one up against its warm body, 'it is difficult for us to understand your point of view. We live rather quiet go-as-you-please lives down here. One day is very like another, and we have no particular rules, and no one has any particular respect paid to him.'

'You all belong to the Lord of Han,' said Lee-Su.

'It makes no ——' began the mouse, but the heron interrupted him.

'Tell us about the place you come from,' it said, 'where the Lord of Han lives; I daresay it is very different from this.'

'Indeed it is,' said Lee-Su, and, thinking of the Palace, he said a piece of poetry about it: 'The gates of my house are built of yellow gold. The hall of my house is paved with white jade.'

'Cree, cree, cree,' said the mouse, 'that would never suit me; cold to the stomach and cruel to the teeth, that's jade.'

'In the great hall sit the harp-players; the incense-burners are lit; a sweet scent fills the air; sweet sounds strike on the ears; the Palace folk go up and down the wide stairs; the Caps and Belts, the Lords in high office, hurry in and out; the Lord of Han sits in his carved chair and drinks wine from a green jade cup.'

'Jade again,' said the mouse.

'Indoor life does not much appeal to me,' said the heron, who had never been inside a house. 'Are the grounds of the Palace pleasant? Is the fishing good?'

'They are very beautiful,' said Lee-Su, and remembering the magnolia trees, and the pagodas and the summer-houses set among the bright flowers, and the green water running under the carved wooden bridges in the Palace garden, he felt for a moment as if the dark night had turned into day; but he thought: 'It is unlikely that I shall ever walk with my companions along those paths again, because the cold has now gone through my skin and my bones, and soon it will reach my heart and freeze it.' However, he belonged to one of the noblest families in the land of Han, and he knew how a gentleman should behave, so he showed no sign of what he was feeling, and turning to the heron with a polite smile, he said, 'the fishing is excellent.'

'I wonder,' began the mouse, 'purely as an interesting speculation, are you really performing your whole duty to your master in waiting for him here? Suppose some disaster has overtaken him in the mountains? Should you not ——?'

'To express such a thought is not respectable,' said Lee-Su. 'My master is the Son of Heaven; no disaster

can overtake him—and in any case—in any case ——'
he found it difficult to speak, he was so cold, and faint
with hunger besides, 'I am not very clever,' he said desperately, 'I am not expected to think for myself, but I
am expected to obey orders, and the order was to wait
here. I have waited, and I am going on waiting.'

'Well,' said the heron, 'as we say in our family, that
is very interesting, but it does not catch fish, and as I see
the dawn is about to break, I must get down to the
river.'

It bowed and walked away. Lee-Su raised his eyes,
and, sure enough, the sky above them was streaked
with saffron and rose-colour, and the little wind which
always comes just before sunrise swept over the Sesura
bushes.

'My master will soon be here now,' said Lee-Su, and
to himself he thought: 'I must stand up, to show that I
am ready for him,' but he was so stiff and frozen that he
could not move hand or foot. 'This is serious,' he thought,
'I must stand on my two feet, and I must put out my lantern before the Lord of Han comes, and I can do neither
of these two things,' He tried again, but he could not
move hand or foot. 'If the Lord of Han comes and finds
me sitting on the ground, if I do not spring to my feet
at the first sight of his approach the shame for my family
will be greater than I can bear.' But he could not move
hand or foot.

'I don't want to meet the Lord of Han, but I should
like just to see him,' said the mouse. 'Tell me when you
see him coming, and I shall hide behind a Sesura bush
and watch.'

'Oh Mouse,' said Lee-Su, 'I am ruined. My family will never hold up their heads again. My father will have to retire to a distant province. None of our friends will know where we are. I have frozen so solid that I cannot rise to my feet to greet my Lord.'

'You do have the most extraordinary troubles,' said the mouse, 'if I had frozen so stiff that I could not move paw or tail, I should not be worrying about lords and families.'

'I ought to have stood up all night,' said Lee-Su, 'I was lazy, and now I am ruined.'

'Well,' said the mouse, 'I don't understand your ideas, but I shall prove to you how useful very small people are—I am too small to be noticed by the Lord of Han, but I am beautifully warm. I shall lie first on your right foot and then on your left, and then on your knees, and in the crook of your elbows and on your wrists, and then when your joints are thawed, my advice to you is to lie flat on the ground and roll the stiffness out of the rest of you.'

It jumped up on to Lee-Su's right foot, and sat on it, and scrabbled it with its little paws—like massaging— and flicked it with its tail, until Lee-Su found he could wriggle his toes and move his ankle—'Oh Mouse, thank you,' he said.

The mouse said nothing, but went quickly to his left foot and did the same to it, and to his knees, and his wrists and elbows, and then Lee-Su lay back on the ground and rolled over and over as the mouse had advised, as hard as he could go, until he was glowing from head to foot, and then he sprang up and put out his lantern, for the first rays of the sun were showing over the mountain top.

'Mouse,' he said, looking down at it—he ached from head to foot but he was so pleased at being able to stand that he hardly noticed the pain—'You have done me a service which will never be forgotten; when I go back to the Palace, I shall have a mouse embroidered on my collar in gold, and so, I think, will the rest of my family, and in this way, because of your good deed, your likeness will always be in the presence of the Lord of Han.'

'You don't seem able to understand the sort of person I am,' said the mouse, 'I really don't care about that kind of thing, but by all means have a gold likeness of me embroidered if it would give you pleasure.' It washed its face with its paws.

'But what can I give you, or what can I do for you that will give *you* pleasure?' asked Lee-Su.

'Nothing,' said the mouse, 'I'm too small.'

But Lee-Su remembered his wallet, and opening it, he found a few crumbs left from the rice cakes which he had given to the horse.

'Will you eat these?' he asked, squatting down, and scattering the crumbs in front of it.

The mouse looked at the crumbs—'I suppose there isn't enough here to do you any good,' it said, 'but for me it is an excellent breakfast. I like cooked food, for once in a way.'

And it ate up all the crumbs, which pleased Lee-Su very much, because he felt he had partly paid his debt.

When he stood up again, he saw two figures in the distance, coming down the side of the mountain. They

'Nothing,' said the mouse, 'I'm too small'

stopped, and saluted each other and parted, and one went up the mountain-side again—the holy Hermit going back to his hut. The other came down towards the plain. It was the Lord of Han.

Lee-Su, the lantern-bearer, stood up straight and stiff; he pulled the staff of his lantern out of the ground and held it over his shoulder with the lantern bob-bob-bobbing on the end of it, which is the correct position in the daytime. The Lord of Han was hidden from sight for a few minutes behind the big boulders, and then he reappeared on the edge of the plain, coming towards them. His horse knew him and whinnied.

The Lord of Han approached the place where he had told his lantern-bearers to wait for him. He looked east and he looked south, but he saw no one except the faithful Lee-Su, holding his reins, ready for him to mount.

The Lord of Han mounted his horse and turned his head in the direction of the Palace. Lee-Su prepared to run at his side. But just before he started, the Lord of Han turned his head a little towards him.

'Are the other lantern-bearers dead?' he asked.

'Chief Star of Heaven, I do not know,' answered Lee-Su in a trembling voice. He had never spoken to the Lord of Han before.

'If they are not dead, they soon will be,' said the Lord of Han.

'Oh, Lord, the night was long and dark, and a dragon came in the darkest hour.'

'If *you* could stay in spite of the cold and darkness and the dragon, why could not they?'

'Oh, Lord it was to me that you gave your horse to

hold. I had the greatest honour. Honour keeps a man warm, and makes a coward brave.'

Lee-Su trembled. The Lord of Han frowned; then he remembered the night he had spent in talking to the holy Hermit about the highest matters, and thoughts of anger and vengeance went out of his mind for the moment.

'*Your* faithfulness is perhaps greater than *their* unfaithfulness,' he said, and he took food out of his silken travelling bag and gave it to Lee-Su, who fell on one knee and ate. When he had finished, the Lord of Han unpinned a dragon brooch of green jade from his collar and bade Lee-Su approach, and, while Lee-Su almost fainted with delight, he fastened it on his breast. Then he gathered up his reins; the sun shone on his embroidered sleeves and on his majestic head. His horse started forward and the happy Lee-Su ran beside it.

When they had disappeared, the mouse came out from under a Sesura bush and began to eat the crumbs of the food which the Lord of Han had given to Lee-Su.

'Dinner comes quickly after breakfast today,' it said, 'really there is something to be said for moving in Court circles.'

The Fox's Daughter

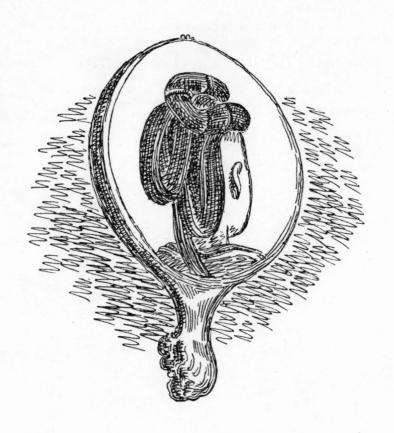

The Fox's Daughter

* 🦊 *

NOTHING is luckier than to be the child of a fox, for, without taking the trouble to learn anything, foxes know as much magic as the man who spends his whole life studying it, and when a fox's child takes human form, as sometimes happens, and becomes a boy or a girl, he knows as much magic as his father.

Liu was a young student who should have been working hard for his examinations, but he was rather idle and much preferred wandering about his father's estate, or sailing in a boat on the river which ran through it, to sitting indoors over his books.

One day, when he was occupied—if it can be called occupied—in this way, he saw the form of a young girl among the reeds which grew upon a little island in the river. Quickly he jumped into his boat and hurried across the water, and, tying the boat up to a willow tree, he began to search the island for her.

For some time he saw nothing, but he heard mocking laughter to the right and to the left, and, running wildly first in one direction and then in the other, he tore his silk robe and broke the strap of one of his sandals. At last he succeeded in running her down, but she looked so beautiful, leaning against a tree and smiling at him, that

Looking at his torn robe and flapping sandal

even after he had got his breath back he could not speak.

'Alas,' said the girl in a clear low voice, looking at his torn robe and flapping sandal, 'if Master Liu pursued his studies with the same zeal as he has pursued me, he would take a high place when the candidates go up to the Examination Hall, and some day he would be a man of great importance—but of course he will do nothing of the sort.'

Liu eagerly asked her name and how she happened to know all about him, and also how she came to be upon the island, for he could see no boat except his own.

'My name is Feng-Lien,' said the maiden, 'but as to how I came here, I shall not tell you, and I can go away again as swiftly.'

(This was not surprising, because of course she was a fox's daughter, and could appear and disappear at will.) And now she made a movement as if she meant to go, but Liu sprang forward with his hands spread out.

'I beg you to stay,' he cried, 'or at least tell me where we shall meet again, for you are the most beautiful person I have ever seen.'

'Look for me in your books,' said the maiden; then, seeing his face become clouded with disappointment, she took a little silver mirror from her girdle and gave it to him. 'There,' she said, 'you shall have something which has belonged to me, but I warn you, you will never see me in it except through your books.' And in a moment she had vanished.

Liu went back to his boat feeling very sad, and many times before he reached the house he looked longingly into the silver mirror, but all he saw was the back-view of the beautiful Feng-Lien standing as if she was watching someone going away from her.

As soon as he reached his room, remembering what she had said, he took out the heavy and difficult books which he had never had a mind to study, and laying them on the top of the mirror, he tried to see it through them, but of course he saw nothing, not even its silver handle, buried under those great volumes.

'Feng-Lien meant more than she said,' he remarked to himself, and he removed the books from the mirror with a sigh and applied himself earnestly to reading them, refusing to see his friends when they came to the house and not accepting any invitations. After he had spent several days in this way, he looked into the mirror again, and there was Feng-Lien with her face turned towards him, smiling and nodding as if she was pleased.

For a month or more he did nothing but study, looking often into the mirror to be encouraged by the lovely face of Feng-Lien, but presently the fine summer weather came, and he could not force himself to stay in the house. He began once more to wander about the garden and the wild land beside the river, idly enjoying the scent of the newly opened flowers and the sight of the bright birds.

'Perhaps I shall see Feng-Lien again,' he said. But he did not find her, and in his heart he knew she would not come while be behaved in this way. Then, one evening after he had been on a fishing expedition all day with some friends, when he pulled out the silver mirror he saw Feng-Lien crying bitterly, and the next morning she had her back turned to him.

'It is clear that there is only one thing to be done,' he

He looked often into the mirror

E

said to himself, 'I must make a habit of working all the time.'

He took the silver mirror and nailed it on the wall so that whenever he raised his eyes from his difficult reading he would see Feng-Lien's face. She always looked happy now. This went on for two years, and at the end of that time he went up to the Examination Hall and did so well that he took a high place in the final list.

'Now,' he said, 'at last, I shall surely be allowed to see Feng-Lien herself.'

He took up the mirror and looked for a long time at her reflection, at the arched eyebrows and the beautiful eyes and the smiling mouth, until it seemed to him that her lips parted and she spoke, yes, she seemed to be speaking words of welcome and congratulation, and suddenly the mirror dissolved into a drop of dew and instead of her likeness, Feng-Lien herself stood before him.

'Really,' she said, bowing very low, 'I am quite frightened of this learned young man.'

'The success I have had is entirely owing to you,' said Liu.

So they were married, and Liu attained to one of the highest positions in China, but Feng-Lien never again had to use the magic she possessed by reason of being a fox's daughter. She found quite simple ways of keeping her husband, who continued to be by nature somewhat lazy, up to the mark.

```
*  *  *  *  *  *  *  *  *  *  *  *  *  *  *  *  *
*                                               *
*              The Toys                         *
*                                               *
*  *  *  *  *  *  *  *  *  *  *  *  *  *  *  *  *
```

The Toys

The Toys

* 🐉 *

L EN-LU was a sailor's daughter. She lived with her
mother in an old house on the waterside of a
Chinese town, and when her father's ship was in
port, he lived there too. They were not rich, but Len-
Lu had a very good time for all that. Her aunt and uncle
kept a shop quite close to her mother's house, where
they sold china and jade and silk embroideries, and as
they had no children they were particularly fond of Len-
Lu, who went to see them nearly every day.

She helped them to set out the jade and ivory carvings
on lacquer trays, and pretended to take a share in polish-
ing the silver and copper bells of which they had a great
number, but she was not expected to do any real work,
because she was only nine years old. It was only a game
to her, and as soon as she grew tired of it she would
wander off and play by herself among the tea-chests and
golden dragons in the upstairs rooms. Her uncle and
aunt allowed her to go wherever she liked because they
knew she would not break or spoil anything. 'She has
the neatest fingers in the world,' they said.

So Len-Lu played at shops and at houses, but best of
all she liked to play she was a sailor like her father, travelling to distant countries. She took a bamboo basket
which was big enough for her to sit in and packed it with

With her hands buried in the sleeves of her coat

a set of ivory draughtsmen and painted fans and little figures made of jade and then got in carefully herself, and waved good-bye to the people on the shore and settled down for the long journey with her hands buried in the sleeves of her coat—for she was the captain and did not have to do any work. But the ship sailed on and on, past the green lotus carvings, through the narrow passage between the big figures of wooden gods, into the clear space of polished floor near the door, where it stopped and she got out and walked about on foreign land. (Really she worked the basket over the slippery floor by pushing with her feet, but she pulled her long coat down so that they hardly showed, and pretended it was done by sailors.) She walked about on foreign land and sold her fans and draughtsmen and then got back into the empty ship and came quickly home with all flags flying and a bundle of money (it was really a lump of ivory tied up in an old scarf) to show to the people who were waiting on the pier beyond the lotus carvings.

That was her favourite game, but sometimes she grew tired of always pretending and then she would stand at the window and look out at the sea and all the real ships in the harbour. There were square-sailed fishing boats, and big junks, like the one her father sailed in, with high prows and gilded figure-heads, and English ships and French ships and Japanese ships, all flying their flags, some being loaded, some being unloaded, some coming in from long voyages, and some just disappearing away out to sea again. And she would stand there for a long time, wishing she could see her father's ship which had broad brown sails with scarlet dragons on them, and wishing that she, too, could put out to sea. So eagerly she watched that her uncle and aunt would call and call before she heard them and came down to her meal of fish and little brightly coloured rice cakes, and tea out of a doll's cup.

And then, one day, sure enough, she saw the ship with the scarlet dragons come sailing between the green headlands into the bay. She did not jump about and wave her arms and shout, because little Chinese girls never show their feelings in those ways, but she went straight downstairs and said to her uncle and aunt: 'My father's ship has come in,' and began to put on the wooden clogs she wore on her bare feet for walking in the streets.

'There is no hurry,' said her uncle, smiling at her, 'it will be hours before they have finished unloading and can come ashore.'

'I shall tell mother, and we'll go down to the pier and watch them,' said Len-Lu. For all her quiet ways, her dark almond-shaped eyes were sparkling with joy.

She said good-bye to her uncle and aunt and found her mother, who was doing the washing in the courtyard behind her house, and told her the news and they went off together to the pier. A good many other people were there already, but they managed to work their way to the front and watched her father's ship being unloaded. After a little while, they caught sight of him and Len-Lu waved, and presently he saw her and waved back, but he had to turn away at once because they were very busy. Then Len-Lu's mother said she must go back to the house to prepare a grand welcome-home meal for her husband, and Len-Lu had to go too, often turning to look back over her shoulder.

That evening they had a lovely time. Her uncle and aunt came in, and when her father had eaten and listened to all the news of home, he began to tell about the adventures of the voyage and the foreign lands he had visited. Len-Lu sat on her cushion beside him with her feet tucked under her and listened and listened without saying a word.

'Len-Lu would like to be a sailor too, I believe,' said her uncle, giving her a candied fig.

'Well,' said her father, 'it's a good life.'

'I should not like to have two sailors in the family,' said her mother, 'for that reason, I am glad Len-Lu is a girl.'

Len-Lu ate her fig and said nothing, but she thought a great many things which she kept to herself.

The next day her father took her down to the ship with him and let her walk about on the deck while he paid the sailors and saw that things were made ready for the next voyage. He was the next in rank to the captain and so he had a great deal to do.

Len-Lu leaned against the deck rail and peeped through the holes in the carving—she was not tall enough to see over it—at the ship which lay next to them in the harbour. It was a big three-decker, all painted white, and flying a French flag. A band was playing on board and tall pale-faced men in white clothes went quickly back and forwards over the wide decks. To Len-Lu the ship seemed like a piece of the foreign lands she longed so much to see, and she stared and stared at it until it was time to go home with her father.

'When will you have a ship of your own?' she asked as they walked to their house.

'As soon as I possibly can save enough money,' said her father. He wanted more than anything in the world to be captain of a ship of his own.

A few days after this, Len-Lu fell ill; not very ill, but ill enough to have to stay indoors all day. She could not even go to her uncle's shop, but when she was getting better he came to see her, and to help her to pass the dull time he taught her to make paper toys. He used the crinkly kind of paper which people in England decorate their rooms with at Christmas time, but he made all sorts of things out of it—pagodas and dragons and flowers, and he fixed them each on two thin sticks to hold them by, and so cunningly that by just giving them a shake the pagodas changed their colour from orange to pink, or white to green, the dragons lashed their tails, and the flowers opened out from small buds into chrysanthemums as big as his hand, and then, at another shake, they went back again as they were at first.

Len-Lu was soon able to make them, too, because she was so neat and quick with her fingers. But all the same she was glad when she was able to get up and go to the ship again with her father.

The time for the next voyage was drawing near. The sailors were busy all day now, the hold was filled with the cargo, the sails were mended and ready; Len-Lu's mother finished the new pair of trousers she was making for her husband and at last the time came when he had to go. He said good-bye to Len-Lu in the house, but he did not notice that she slipped out of the room immediately afterwards and went into the court-yard where his luggage was waiting to be carried to the ship. It was in two big bamboo baskets, tied on either end of a bamboo pole which he would carry across his shoulder. Len-Lu lifted the canvas covering of the baskets and saw that they were not full right up to the top. She quickly took some of the things out of one and put them in the other until it was nearly full, drew the cover over it neatly, and then went back to the first basket which now had only a few soft clothes at the bottom, and jumped in. She curled herself up as she used to do when she played at being a sailor in the basket at her uncle's house, and pulled the canvas cover over her head.

Presently her father came out of the house; he raised the pole and put it across his shoulder, and she heard him give a little surprised grunt when he found it heavier than he had expected. However, he did not imagine that anything was wrong with it, and he set off to the ship without an idea that he was taking his daughter with him. The baskets joggled up and down on the ends of the springy bamboo, and it was quite dark for Len-Lu under the canvas cover; she folded her hands together under the sleeves of her coat, just as she always did when she was playing her game, but now she did not need to work with her feet in order to move her ship. She sat quite still. They went along the narrow street and then took the sharp turn to the left for the jetty. A little boat was waiting there to take her father to his ship. He climbed in and set the baskets down carefully beside him, but when they came to the big ship there was a rather anxious moment for Len-Lu, because, as no one knew there was anything except clothes and other belongings in the basket, the sailors were not particularly careful as to how they held it when they were getting it up the steep side of the ship. She did not know for a moment whether she was right side up or not, or in which direction the sky was and which the sea. But she sat quite still and kept her hands folded, and, luckily for her, her father called to the sailors to be careful, as the covers were not sewn on the baskets and he did not want to see his clothes fall into the harbour. He little knew that his daughter might have fallen in there too.

They carried the baskets into his cabin and set them down and everyone went away to take his share in getting the ship out to sea. Len-Lu sat quietly with the canvas cover still over her head. She did not dare to stir until she felt the ship moving, in case they sent her home again. She heard the captain and her father shouting and the sailors singing as they pulled on the ropes, and at last she felt the ship bound forward under a fair wind, all sails set for a foreign land.

She pushed back the canvas cover and crept out, blinking in the sudden light, but calm and composed as ever, and when her father came in some time later he got the greatest shock he had ever had, for a voice said 'Father!' and, looking up, he saw his daughter standing there in her black coat with her hands clasped in front of her. At first he thought something terrible must have happened to her or to his wife, and that she was a vision, come to tell him of it, but when she smiled and held out her hands he knew she was real, and when he noticed the thrown-back cover of the bamboo basket, he understood what she had done and knew that he had his daughter with him at sea.

What to do about it he did not know. The ship could not put back now or they would lose the good wind which was taking them so quickly over the first stages of their voyage; nor would scolding her be very useful. So he decided to take her to the captain to ask for his orders, and they went off hand in hand. The captain looked very surprised when he saw a little girl on his ship and he frowned in a frightening way when her father told him the story, but at the end of it he suddenly began to laugh.

'So you wanted to be a sailor!' he said, turning his long black moustaches on Len-Lu. 'Well, since you came with us you must stay with us. But do not forget that you must be good and quiet.'

Len-Lu nodded; it was not difficult for her to promise that, because she always was good and quiet.

'So that is settled,' said her father when they were alone again, 'but all the same, you do not seem to have considered other people's feelings as you should. What do you suppose your mother and your kind uncle and aunt are thinking now? They believe you are lost, and probably drowned.'

'No,' said Len-Lu, and she explained that she had left a message which her uncle, who was used to her way of telling him things, for she could not write, would understand and explain to the others. She had set her bamboo boat in the middle of the lumber room where she played, and in it she had laid a piece of paper cut out and coloured like the French flag, and a button from her father's coat and a scrap of her own hair screwed up in a twist of stuff from an old jacket. The button stood for her father, the hair for herself, and the French flag for foreign lands, and her uncle would know that the message meant, 'we have gone on a voyage together.'

'He will be a clever man if he guesses that,' said her father, but Len-Lu insisted that he would read her meaning at once.

And then the lovely days began for Len-Lu. They had the most wonderful weather on that voyage; the good wind stayed with them, the sun shone over the blue sea, the ship sailed through the narrow passages between the white islands where terrible storms have usually to be faced, without encountering anything more frightening than flying fish and dolphins. The sailors said Len-Lu had brought the good luck, and even the captain said once that if she could not pull her weight upon a rope at least she had done something to pay for her passage in arranging the weather so nicely. They were all fond of her, and she helped them in whatever ways she could, such as mending their clothes, for she sewed very neatly. They told her stories and let her go wherever she liked on the ship. She would stand for hours staring through the holes in the carving of the deck rail at the blue sea, flecked with white waves which never broke; sometimes she saw another Chinese junk and sometimes a foreign ship, and every now and then they passed near enough to the shore for her to see strange houses and trees, looking tiny because of the distance. In the evenings she sat beside her father under the lantern in their sleeping place,

Then the lovely days began for Len-Lu

and while he smoked and dreamed about the days when he would be a captain, she passed the time by making dragons and pagodas and chrysanthemums out of crinkly paper which a sailor had given her, in the way her uncle had taught her when she was ill. And, later, when the lantern was put out she would lie in her little bunk and listen to the sea making a sleepy sound on the other side of the wooden wall, and wish it was morning so that she could run quickly up on deck again.

Day after day went by like this, but at last they sighted land. Len-Lu stood beside the sailors on the deck and they all watched the green hills and the white houses draw nearer and nearer to them—it seemed as if it was the land and not the ship that was moving. Lee-Song, a special friend of Len-Lu's who had made this voyage many times, stood near her, and when they had drawn still closer he pointed out the different buildings in the great town and told her what they were.

'Would you like to come ashore with me?' he asked, 'I shall be free to go before your father is.' Len-Lu said she would like it very much if her father gave his permission.

'I was thinking,' went on Lee-Song, who was a clever man and knew that the common things in one country are rare in another, 'that it would be a good thing if you took with you the paper toys you have been making on the voyage to sell to the people in the town. They have never seen anything like your dragons and pagodas.'

Len-Lu shook her head; she was too shy, she did not believe her toys were good enough to sell to anybody.

'Just as you like,' said Lee-Song, 'I am going to take

my carvings'—he did very clever wood-carvings when it
was not his turn for duty at sea—'and I shall come back
to the ship with a lot of money in my handkerchief. But
do just as you like, so far as your toys are concerned.'

Len-Lu remembered the ivory ball she used to tie up
in a scarf and play was the money she had made, in her
games in her uncle's warehouse, and she thought how
splendid it would be and how like a real sailor and not
just a passenger to come back to her ship with money in
a handkerchief. So, although she still felt very shy, she
nodded her head this time instead of shaking it.

'That is right,' said Lee-Song.

He brought a flat bamboo basket with a lid and they
went below to her father's sleeping-place and packed it
with the paper toys and fastened the lid carefully over
them and Lee-Song took charge of it. Len-Lu hoped he
would not tell any of the other sailors what she was going to do, but she was too shy to ask him not to, and
went away and stood beside her father while the ship
moved slowly to its place against the wharf. The brown
sails with the red dragons were furled; the flag flew at
the mast-head. On the shore people said to each other
'Oh, do look at that curious ship! What is it?' And the
ones who knew said, 'it is a Chinese trading junk.' The
ship had come safely to France.

The captain shouted his orders, the sailors ran quickly
over the decks; everyone was in a bustle and fuss. But
presently Lee-Song came to Len-Lu's side.

'I am allowed to go ashore now,' he said, 'Are you
coming?'

Len-Lu looked up at her father and when he nodded

to her, too busy to take much notice, she went off with Lee-Song.

They climbed down the ladder on to the wharf and went up the busy street which led into the centre of the town. It was a fine day and a great many people were about. Len-Lu stared and stared with all her eyes at the strange faces and the strange clothes. Even the buildings were strange to her, and the noises, and the very smells were different from the ones she was used to in her own country. She held on to the edge of Lee-Song's blue tunic with one hand for fear she would lose the last familiar thing she had. When a tram came round the corner suddenly, she almost forgot about never showing her feelings, and did in fact give one little gasp, because just for a second she thought it was a live dragon with people sitting in its inside. It was almost too exciting. But Lee-Song marched cheerfully along, knowing the place well, and enjoying being on shore again. He halted when he came to a place where people were sitting at small round tables eating and drinking out in the street. It was a fashionable restaurant, and as it was just about twelve o'clock, most of the tables were occupied.

'Now!' he said, smiling at Len-Lu, opening the basket of toys and setting it at her feet. 'Here is a good place for you to stand. Take some of the toys in your hands and show how they work. I shall go over to the other side of the tables, not far away, with my carvings. And, Len-Lu, when they ask you how much there is to pay, you must hold up one finger, like this.' (In that way everyone would know that they had to pay one franc each for a toy.)

Lee-Song went over to the other side of the tables and unwrapped his carvings. Len-Lu picked up a dragon, holding the two sticks in her hands to make him lash his tail and shake his head back and forwards. She was very shy and rather frightened as well, but she did not show any of her feelings in her face.

Soon the people sitting at the nearest table saw her—'Why, look! There's a Chinese baby!' they said, 'isn't she sweet?' They thought Len-Lu was younger than she was because she was so small—'What has she got in her hand?' asked the little boy at the table, 'Oh, look, Oh look!' For Len-Lu now took up a chrysanthemum branch and shook the buds out into flowers and back again into buds. The little boy screamed with delight.

'Is she selling them?' asked his mother.

'I'll ask her,' said his father, and he got up and came across to Len-Lu.

He looked very big and terrifying, striding towards her, the white-faced foreign man, but she did not budge, and when he said, in French, because he could not speak Chinese: 'Are you selling these pretty things, my child?' she held up her finger as Lee-Song had told her, hoping that would be a right answer to whatever he had said.

'One franc!' he said, 'Come over here, Etienne, and choose which you want!'

The little boy came up eagerly, and his father not only bought him whatever he asked for, but he chose a pagoda for himself and a chrysanthemum branch for his wife, and when he went back to his table they both played with them, making the pagoda change colour and

'Oh, look, Oh look!' said the little boy

the chrysanthemums open and shut, and enjoying it as if they were children themselves.

Soon the people at the other tables noticed them. What is it? Where did they get those things? Can't we have one? they asked each other, and then they saw Len-Lu with her basket, and immediately someone came from every table to buy for the rest, they were all so eager to have one of the pretty toys to play with as they sat in the sun listening to the band and eating their lunch. Lee-Song had to come over to help her, it all went so fast, and the money was hard for her to handle. 'Dear little thing!' the foreign people said—there were English and Americans there as well as French—'Oh, really she is a darling!' and although Len-Lu did not understand their language she knew they were all friendly and liked her toys, and she enjoyed herself enormously as she handed out dragons and pagodas and chrysanthemums and showed them how they ought to be shaken, and smiled and smiled.

At last the basket was quite empty and Lee-Song's carvings were all sold.

'We must go back to the ship,' he said, but first he put Len-Lu's money in a handkerchief and tied it with a hard knot and gave it to her to carry. 'Hold it tight,' he said. He need not have worried, because she was far too proud and happy to run any risk of losing it.

'Would you like to use some of your money to ride back to the ship in one of those things?' he asked, pointing to a tram, but Len-Lu shook her head. She wanted her father to untie the knot in the handkerchief himself and see all the money she had made for him—every penny of it.

He was even more surprised and pleased when he saw it than she could have hoped.

'This means more than you think,' he said, getting up and walking back and forwards in his excitement. 'It has given me a good idea. Len-Lu, would you like to come with me on all my voyages?'

'I think you know that I have always wanted to go to sea,' said Len-Lu.

'I guessed it when I knew you had come aboard in my clothes basket!' said her father.

'And I like it even better than I thought I would,' she said.

'Well then, listen, Len-Lu,' said her father, 'when we get home, I shall sell our house and with that money and what we shall save by not having any housekeeping on shore, I shall be able to afford to buy a ship, and your mother and you will come with me on all my voyages, and when we are in China we shall stay with your uncle and aunt. Thus I shall be a captain long before I expected, and you will pay for your passage by making these toys and selling them in the foreign lands we visit. Len-Lu,' he added tenderly, 'You have made your family's fortune.' And that is exactly what happened.

```
* * * * * * * * * * * * * * * * * *
*                                 *
*  In the Far South-West          *
*                                 *
* * * * * * * * * * * * * * * * * *
```

In the Far South-West

In the Far South-West

* 🜲 *

KU-LING was ten years old when his family fell on bad times. His father was ill, and no matter what medicines he took, he did not get better. As he could not work, he became very poor, and he and Ku-Ling and Ku-Ling's mother and sister had to leave their house with lattice-work gates, and the garden full of dwarf flowering peach trees and ponds with gold-fish, and go to live in a hut with a plain door back and front, no land, and very little to put in the pot.

Ku-Ling used to think for hours at a time what could be done to better their condition, but without having a single idea. Then one night when he was asleep a small person in a red cap and red trousers appeared to him in a dream and said, 'your father will be cured by water from the river in the Country of Sleep.'

'Where is the Country of Sleep?' asked Ku-Ling, 'How can I get there?'

'Go far into the South-west,' said the small person, 'and then inquire the way.'

As he said these words he vanished, and Ku-Ling fell into an ordinary sleep. But he did not forget what had happened, and the next morning he put on his travelling coat and filled a large bag with food. He said good-bye to his father and to the singing-bird which was the last of all the pretty things that had once been his, and putting his baby sister out of his way, he went to the door. His mother ran after him and asked where he was going.

'I am going to get a cure for my father's illness,' said Ku-Ling. 'Do not be distressed. I have had a good dream; I know what I am about.'

But his mother thought only that another misfortune had befallen her and that her dear son was bewitched, for she did not in the least believe that he could find a cure for her husband, and she wept and wailed long after Ku-Ling had disappeared round the bend of the road.

Ku-Ling put into the pocket in his sleeve the bottle he had brought for the water from the Country of Sleep and set out at a good pace. All day he walked in the direction of the South-west, but when it got dark he was so tired that he could go no farther without rest, and he lay down to sleep under a Japonica tree. Now it happened that two very powerful good spirits were sitting in the tree. They could turn themselves into anything they liked and at the moment they were in the form of birds.

'That is Ku-Ling asleep down there,' said one of them. 'He is a good boy. He is going all the way to the Country of Sleep to get water to cure his father's illness.'

'Yes,' said the other, 'it is a long way for a boy. To-morrow morning I shall help him. I shall turn myself into a tiger and carry him as far as the borders of the Country of the Feathery People—farther than that I cannot go.'

'Farther than that you cannot go,' agreed the other, 'but even that will greatly shorten his journey.'

So, next morning, before Ku-Ling had taken many

paces he saw a tiger standing in front of him in the road, and before he had time to feel frightened it said: 'Do not be alarmed, Ku-Ling. The object of your journey is known to me and I approve of it. Get on my back and I will shorten the way to the far South-west for you.'

Ku-Ling thought it wisest to do as the tiger advised, so he wound the skirt of his travelling coat tightly round him and sat down on its back and clasped his arms round its neck. In one minute they had covered a hundred miles, in two minutes two hundred, and at the end of an hour they were in the far South-west.

The country was flat and quite bare; no hills, no trees, no water, but in the distance he could see two huge iron gates which seemed to be fixed in the sky.

'This,' said the tiger, coming to a standstill, 'is the far South-west and I can take you no farther. You are on the borders of the Country of the Feathery People. Be polite and steadfast and you will succeed.'

'I was told in my dream to inquire the way when I had reached the far South-west,' said Ku-Ling after he had thanked the tiger for carrying him.

'Yes,' said the tiger, 'and I will tell you. Beyond the Country of the Feathery People lies the Country of the People of the Flying Carts, and beyond that, there where you see those high gates in the distance, is the Country of Giants, and on the other side of that is the small Country of the Pigmy People, and on the far side of that again stretches the Country of Sleep. The way there will be long, but if you behave correctly the way back will be short.'

The tiger then vanished and Ku-Ling set out to walk

He clasped his arms round its neck

across the great plain. For a long time he saw no sign of life, but presently he made out the shapes of some tall people in the distance; they were standing together in a group, but what they were doing he could not see. For a little while he thought they were Giants, and was rather alarmed at the idea of coming upon them before he had braced himself up to enter their country, but as he drew nearer he saw that they were indeed the Feathery People. They were shaped like men and women, but their bodies were covered with fine down and they had wings instead of arms. When he had come quite close to them he realized that there was no need to be afraid, for, on catching sight of him, they ran away as fast as they could, and even flew for short distances, rather heavily and clumsily, like hens.

Ku-Ling held out his hands to show that he was on a peaceful errand, but although they kept turning to look back and were evidently curious about him, they were also extremely timid, and it was some time before they decided to let him catch up with them.

When he stood beside them he saw that they were all about seven or eight feet high, and had very long beaky noses, but their faces were gentle and shy. 'Why have you come here?' asked the one who seemed to be the leader of the group, in a soft hesitating voice.

'I wish to pass through your country in order to get water from the river in the Country of Sleep, to cure my father's illness,' said Ku-Ling politely.

'The Country of Sleep, the Country of Sleep, now where is that?' they asked, looking at each other in surprise. 'We have never heard of it.'

93

'It lies beyond your country and beyond the People of the Flying Carts, and beyond the Giants and the Pigmies,' said Ku-Ling.

'Oh dear, Oh dear,' they said in a soft chorus, 'it is very far away. We are afraid you will never come back,' and being very tender-hearted, they began to weep.

'Do not weep for me,' said Ku-Ling, 'I know by signs from good spirits that I shall be successful. But I should be glad if you would show me where to find some water, because I do not see any rivers in your land, and I am very thirsty.'

'Alas, alas,' they said sadly, 'we have no water in our land. We always drink milk, because it is better for our voices.'

'I, too, drink milk when I can get it,' said Ku-Ling, after waiting in vain for them to offer him some.

Immediately they became more cheerful and one of them went off at a great pace, sometimes running, sometimes breaking into a short flight, to one of their villages which Ku-Ling now saw in the shelter of a large rock. Soon he came back with a large pail of milk, followed by many other Feathery People who watched with great interest as Ku-Ling drank the milk and opened his bag of food. He offered to share his rice cakes with them, but they shook their heads.

'No, no,' they said nervously, 'food of that kind would spoil our voices. We never eat anything but eggs.'

'I am sorry I have none to offer you,' said Ku-Ling.

'We have plenty,' said one of them. 'We have everything we need.'

When he said this the others laughed and nodded

Ku-Ling held out his hands

their heads and became almost merry. 'Yes, yes, we have everything we need,' they said, 'and now perhaps you would like us to sing to you?'

'I should like it very much,' said Ku-Ling politely.

At once they gathered round their leader and began to sing, and Ku-Ling realized that this was what they had been doing when he first saw them. The sound echoed far over the great plain, rising and falling, marvellously sweet, for their voices were lovelier than any he had ever heard. He could have sat there for long enough listening to them, but the sun was setting, and, although he felt very tired, he remembered his errand, and rose and began to go forward towards the Country of the People of the Flying Carts. The Feathery People closed round him in a great semi-circle and walked with him, still singing as sweetly as ever, but now more sadly, until they came to a low ridge in the plain, which, although it did not seem very high, hid the flat country on the other side of it from sight. It was the boundary of their land. They stopped at once and bowed to Ku-Ling, who bowed to them and thanked them for their kindness. Seeing him go forward and leave them they began to weep, but soon they turned back into their own country and as he climbed the ridge he heard their sweet singing dying away in the distance.

As soon as he had climbed to the top of the ridge he lost the sound of their voices, and, what was more surprising, he lost all feeling of tiredness. He felt strong and able to walk for miles, as if he had just risen from a good night's sleep, and, looking at the sky, he saw that the sun, which had been about to set in the Country of the

Feathery People had just risen here. It was the same kind of rocky waterless plain, and there were no trees, but here and there were what looked like flagpoles, without flags, stuck up in the sand and painted in bright colours, red, blue, green and orange.

Ku-Ling walked on and on, enjoying the fine morning air, glad that he felt so strong and brisk; he had forgotten all about the inhabitants of the country and was thinking more about the Giants, whose land was the next he would have to pass through, when he heard a loud shout which seemed to come from over his head. He looked up, but could see nothing except what he took to be a flock of swallows, wheeling and circling gracefully at a great height. Soon, however, they came down lower and grew larger than any swallows could be, and presently he made out that they were really brightly painted carts, with wheels and shafts, exactly like the carts which were used in his own country, and in them sat people with flags in their hands which they waved continually as they shouted across to each other from cart to cart. But they had seen Ku-Ling, and as it seemed they had only to wish in order to make the carts go wherever they pleased, they soon alighted close to him on the ground. The carts came down so cleverly they did not even bump as they touched the earth, and their occupants at once climbed out and came towards Ku-Ling, who saw then that all of them, both men and women, had but one arm apiece, in which they grasped their flags.

'Who are you, and what do you want here?' they asked, clustering round him.

'I am Ku-Ling, going to the Country of Sleep to get a

cure for my father's illness,' said Ku-Ling politely, 'and I ask permission to pass through your land.'

'The Country of Sleep!' they exclaimed, and immediately began to shout with laughter. 'What a horrible country that must be! Now we hardly ever go to sleep, and we wish we never did. It is such a waste of time when we might be flying. Flying is the best thing in the world, don't you agree?'

'It must be pleasant on such a fine morning as this,' said Ku-Ling.

'But it is always a fine morning here!' they cried, and they waved their flags and began to jump about, laughing and sporting together in the gayest manner.

They were merry people and Ku-Ling would have liked well enough to stay with them for a time, but he remembered his errand and thought of his poor father lying ill at home, and so he said, 'with your permission I will now continue my journey. I have still to pass through the Land of Giants and the Pigmy country, for the Country of Sleep lies on the far side of them both.'

'You are going through the Land of the Giants?' they asked, sobering down for a moment, and one of them added, 'I hardly know how that is to be done. You see those great gates over there?' he asked, pointing with his flag, 'well, they are easy to open on the Giants' side, but impossible to open on this side. That is the boundary between our country and theirs and we have never passed beyond it. Sometimes the Giants come into our country to find out whether the People of the Flying Carts are good to eat, but they don't catch us, because we are careful to fly round and round just beyond the

reach of their arms. It is quite a good sport.' And he began to laugh again, thinking of the fun they had with the
Giants.

'But could you not fly over their gates, if you wanted
to?' asked Ku-Ling.

'We can't fly as high as that,' they said.

'Could you not get in at either side of the gates?'
asked Ku-Ling. 'There does not seem to be any wall; I
can see nothing but the sky.'

'Nothing but the sky! That is a good joke,' they
shouted. 'No, indeed there is nothing but the sky, but
that sky is a wall as solid as rock and so high that no man
has ever seen its top.'

'I must try to get in, all the same,' said Ku-Ling, 'and
I do not give up hope, because I have been warned by
good spirits that I shall be successful.'

'Come flying with us for a little while first,' said one
of them. 'We can lend you a flag, although we have
never had time to make enough for the flag poles we
put up.'

And they all begged him to come flying with them.
But Ku-Ling shook his head, because he was afraid too
much time would be wasted. Then one of the women
had a good idea: 'Why should we not fly with him to the
borders of the Giants' country?' she asked. 'We don't
mind in what direction we go, so long as we are flying,
and it would shorten his journey.'

The others gladly agreed, and Ku-Ling, thanking
them, climbed into the cart beside the woman who had
made the offer. She put a flag into his hands and they
set off.

The carts went straight up into the air, but so easily that it was not possible to tell from the motion at what minute they left the earth. Then they wheeled round in a half-circle and set out for the great gates in the distance, and all the merry people, who became even merrier when they were in the air, shouted back and forwards to each other and waved their gay flags. Ku-Ling waved his too, because he wished to show them that he appreciated their kindness. He used both hands as the staff was rather heavy, but after a little while the woman whose cart he was in asked him if he would mind using one hand only and hiding the other as much as possible in his sleeve, because she had never seen anyone with two hands before and it made her feel uncomfortable; so after this he used only one hand like the rest of them.

The carts went very fast and it was not long before they had arrived at the Giants' gates set in solid sky. Here they came down to earth again and the people said good-bye to Ku-Ling.

'We are sorry you are going,' they said. 'If you had stayed with us, we would have made you a little cart of your own, and if by some means you had managed to get rid of that extra arm you have, you might have been one of us.'

'I should have liked nothing better,' said Ku-Ling politely, 'but as it is I must think of my father. Thank you very much for your kind help.'

Then they jumped into their carts again, and waving their flags for good-bye, they soon vanished into the distance and looked like nothing but a flock of swallows wheeling and circling gracefully about.

Ku-Ling set his hand against the blue sky on either side of the great gates and found that it was cold and solid to the touch, like glass or ice. There was no more hope of passing through it than there is of passing through glass or ice. Then he looked at the great gates, which were so tall that now he was close up to them he could not see their tops. They were made of thick iron rods, clamped with thick iron bands, but when he looked at them carefully his spirits rose, because, since they had been made to keep out the people of the Flying Carts who were all eight feet tall and about three feet across the shoulders, the bars were set fairly widely apart, and as he himself was going to be a man of only the ordinary Chinese size and had not yet got his full growth, he thought that he might manage to slip between them if he turned sideways. So he pulled his coat very tightly round him and laid his bag of food on the ground close to the bars, and making himself as small as he could he wriggled and wriggled, and sure enough, he came out on the other side. Then he drew his bag through the bars by its straps and with his heart beating rather quickly, set out to cross the Giants' country.

It seemed to him at first that he had come into a mountainous land, for he saw a high black ridge on his right, but when he looked at it more closely he saw, high up, the glitter of glass and higher up still, puffs of smoke, not coming up from one hole like a volcano, but strung out in a line, 'as if it came from chimneys', he thought, and then he realized that it did come from chimneys, and that the glitter of glass meant windows, and that what he had taken for a ridge of mountains was a row of enormous houses. He tried to walk quickly, but the Giants' country was very big, and even the pebbles in the path were as large as good-sized stones in his own land, and the grass was like tall reeds, and so he could not get on very fast.

As he was working his way through a patch of grass which was so high that he could hardly see over the top, he heard a rumbling sound and, peeping between the grass stems, he saw a monstrous carriage coming towards him drawn by a monstrous horse. The animal was so big that it was only by craning his neck that he could see its head, and as for the man who was driving it, at first he thought he was a blue hill, he was so enormous. He must have been quite eighty feet high; the blue blouse he wore would have served for a tent for Ku-Ling and all his relations, and the belt which went round it could not have been raised from the ground by Ku-Ling's father even when he was in his full strength. His eyebrows were so long that they stuck out over the front of the cart, and his voice as he encouraged his horse sounded like thunder in the hills.

'There is only one thing that may save me,' said Ku-Ling to himself, as the carriage came up to him, 'perhaps I am so small that he cannot see me.'

But the Giant's eyes were very good, and he glanced sharply at the patch of waving grass where Ku-Ling stood, and then, quick as light, stretched his leg out of the cart and caught him up between his toes (he had bare feet) and lifted him into the cart.

Ku-Ling held himself quite still between the Giant's first and second toes because he was afraid that if he

moved he would press him more tightly, which meant
that he would be pinched black and blue all over, but
the Giant plucked him quite gently from between his
toes with his finger and thumb and held him close up to
his face to examine him. He seemed as surprised by
Ku-Ling as Ku-Ling was by him. His great eyes, which
seemed to Ku-Ling as big as basins, grew bigger still as he
stared at him, but he did not seem to wish him any harm,
because when he spoke he made his voice as soft as
possible so that the draught from his breath would not
blow him away; even so, it was like standing in a strong
wind.

'Who are you, and where do you come from?' asked
the Giant.

'I am Ku-Ling, going to the Country of Sleep to fetch
a cure for my father's illness, and I beg you to give me
permission to pass through your land,' said Ku-Ling.

He spoke as loudly as he could, but the Giant had to
ask him to repeat himself and to hold him up against his
ear before he could hear what he said.

'What!' he exclaimed at last, 'can creatures as small
as you fall ill? I do not see how there is room for an illness inside such a little body. Is your father as small as
you are?' he asked.

'He is taller than I am,' said Ku-Ling, 'because I am
only a boy, but I doubt whether the difference in our
sizes would be great enough to be noticed by you,
Honourable Sir.'

'And he is ill, you say, and you are going to fetch him
a cure—is that what you said?' asked the Giant.

'Yes, Honourable Sir,' said Ku-Ling.

'Can creatures as small as you fall ill?'

'Well it is lucky for you that it was I who found you, and not one of my brothers and sisters,' said the Giant, 'because I alone of all of them know what it is to be ill, and it makes me feel pity for your father. If my brothers and sisters saw you,' he went on, 'I do not think they would eat you, because you are too small to be worth the trouble of cooking, but they might keep you as a toy, or they might kill you for coming into our country. I am quite sure they would not give you permission to pass through it. That is never allowed.'

'But you, Honourable Sir, will have more kindness. than they ——' began Ku-Ling pleadingly.

'They are always telling me that I am hardly fit to be one of them because I suffer from a weak stomach,' said the Giant sadly. 'And I suppose they are right, but I must say I feel pity for your father when I hear that he is ill. I was in great pain for two hours after breakfast today,' he added, 'although I had eaten only two oxen, while all the others, even my youngest sister, who is scarcely grown up, had six apiece.'

'If I get to the Country of Sleep and find the water which will cure my father, I shall bring some away for you, too,' said Ku-Ling.

The Giant was so much touched by this suggestion that tears came into his eyes and one fell on Ku-Ling, wetting him from head to foot.

'Very well,' he said, 'I shall drive you to the other side of our country, and I shall not tell anybody about you. But mind, you must be very careful, for it will take me two days to get to the gates on the far side, and we shall have to spend the night in a house belonging to a brother and sister-in-law of mine. They would think it strange if I travelled day and night, from one end of the country to the other, without giving any reason.'

'I shall be careful not to be seen,' said Ku-Ling, who now knew that the good spirits had been guiding him, or he would hardly have found the one Giant who could help him.

'You had better climb into my pocket while I am driving,' said the Giant, 'or the wind we make might blow you away, and when we go into the houses I think you had better lie down inside my snuff-box. I shall empty the snuff away and make a hole in the lid for you to breathe through.'

So they set off. Ku-Ling was warm and comfortable in the Giant's pocket, and every now and then, for as long as he was able to bear the great wind of their passage, he peeped over the rim and looked at the country. He saw flocks of giant sheep, and giant flowers, single peonies as big as whole gardens in his own country, and rose bushes taller than willow trees, while the heads of the trees themselves were so high that he could not see them at all. Once they passed some enormous people playing together and the ball that they tossed back and forwards was as big as a balloon.

'My eldest brother's children,' said the Giant, nodding and waving to them, while Ku-Ling quickly drew his head down into the pocket again.

All day they drove through the country, and at night the Giant checked the horse and climbed down in front of one of the huge houses. 'We must spend the night here,' he said, taking Ku-Ling out of his pocket, gently so as not to bruise him, and putting him in his snuff box. 'See, this will do for a bed for you,' and he plucked the down of a thistle which grew at the edge of the road.

Ku-Ling stretched himself out on the thistle-down and was comfortable enough, although the Giant rather jolted him when he walked. It was like being in bed in a cabin at sea.

He heard the thunderous noise of the Giant's brother and sister-in-law welcoming him, and the sound of them drawing their chairs up to table deafened him for a few minutes, but he soon recovered and ate some of his own rice cakes inside the snuff-box. He would have liked to see what the Giant's house looked like inside, but he was really glad to be so safe. He only had one dangerous minute in the house, and that was when the giant took out his snuff-box and was just going to open it to have a pinch of snuff when he remembered about Ku-Ling.

'I am afraid, brother, you will have to give me a pinch from your box,' he said, 'I forgot to fill mine up this morning. It is quite empty,' and he put Ku-Ling back safely into his pocket again.

The next morning their start was rather delayed by the Giant's stomach-ache, which came upon him very violently, after breakfast. His brother and sister-in-law were not at all sorry for him; in fact they laughed heartily when he was roaring with pain, because they had not the least idea what it felt like.

'But *you* know what it is like,' said the Giant, when at last they were in the carriage and Ku-Ling was peeping over the edge of his pocket again. 'Tell me, is your father as ill as I am?'

'He is worse than you are,' said Ku-Ling, 'because your pain passes and you are better again until the next time, but my father can never rise from his bed.'

'I am really sorry for your father,' said the Giant, urging the horse to go faster so that Ku-Ling would the sooner reach the Country of Sleep where he was to get the cure.

They drove and drove, and at last they came to a pair of great gates set in solid sky exactly like the ones which Ku-Ling had come in by on the other side of the country.

'We never go out on this side,' said the Giant, 'but as we had gates at the one end, our forefathers thought it was neater to have some at this end as well—which is very lucky for you.'

'It is indeed,' said Ku-Ling, wondering about the Pigmy People who he had been told lived on the far side of the Giants' country.

'Here I must say good-bye,' said the Giant, lifting Ku-Ling very gently out of his pocket and setting him on the ground. 'Wait, I shall open the gate for you.'

He put his great hand on the gate and it opened as easily as the lattice front door of Ku-Ling's old house used to open when his father came home in the evening. Then Ku-Ling tried to thank the Giant for all his kindness, but although he put his hands round his mouth and shouted as loudly as he could, the Giant shook his head.

'I can't hear you,' he said, 'but never mind. Only, if you do find the cure for your father, I shall be glad if you spare some for me.'

He shut the gate and sprang into his carriage again,

and Ku-Ling started forward into the new country beyond the wall of sky.

There was a narrow strip of flat land and then a broad
line of high trees. And the appearance of the trees made
Ku-Ling feel that at last he was drawing near to the Country of Sleep, for, although they were alive, and some of
them were even in flower, they looked different from
any he had seen, and yet he knew their various kinds well
enough—there was just the difference between them
and the trees he knew at home that there is between a
person's face when he is awake and when he is asleep.
The trees were all fast asleep.

Ku-Ling was stepping quickly towards them when suddenly he felt a weight on the front of one of his feet, and,
looking down, he saw a dozen or so little men and
women were sitting on it, holding on desperately to the
lacing of his sandal and trying to attract his attention. So
he lifted them up in his hand as the Giant had lifted him,
and held them against his ear.

They were the Pigmy People and they were very
much annoyed with him for walking into their country
without permission.

Ku-Ling explained what his errand was, but they were
still angry; they said they did not know where the Country of Sleep was, and that he would tread whole towns of
theirs under foot if he went on in the way he was going.

Ku-Ling said he was very sorry, and set them down on
the ground again and bent down with his hands on his
knees and looked carefully at the ground. Then he saw
that it really was a town, built for people only six inches
high, with shops and temples and houses and a market

He saw a dozen or so little men and women

place. The little people were swarming into the streets to look at him. They were shaped in every way like ordinary men and women and they seemed to do everything that ordinary people do in towns, especially work in jewellery, for he saw a great many jewellers' shops, and they even showed him some of their finished work, but it was too small for him to see properly, and he was afraid to pick it up and bring it close to his eyes for fear he broke it.

The question was how he was to cross their country; he did not want to break their towns, and yet he must get to the Country of Sleep. Looking carefully over the pieces of ground which separated him from the sleepy trees, he saw several open spaces which seemed to him large enough to hold one of his feet, and picking up a little man, he asked him what these were and he learned that they were grazing grounds for their sheep, and public parks.

'Then,' said Ku-Ling, 'will you give orders for the sheep to be driven out of each of them for a little while, and I shall step carefully from one to the other and so go out of your country without hurting anything.'

'It will take a little time,' said the Pigmy man, 'for I must send runners from here to the farther grounds to take the message to the shepherds. It is no use for you to raise your voice to shout to them. They would only think it was thunder, or be too much afraid to do anything.'

'Very well,' said Ku-Ling, and to pass the time until the runners came back with the message that the sheep had been moved, he took out one of his rice cakes and began to eat. Instantly all the little people in the streets of the town put up their umbrellas to protect themselves from the falling crumbs, but when his meal was over they put down their umbrellas and pulled the crumbs into their houses and had a great feast.

Presently the runners returned and said that it would now be safe for him to step in the green spaces, but that he must go very carefully and kilt up the skirts of his coat so that they did not drag the roofs off the houses which lay in his way. So Ku-Ling said good-bye to the Pigmy People and went very carefully from one little green space to the next. It was like walking on stepping stones across a brook. In a minute or two he was in among the sleeping trees on the edge of the Country of Sleep.

And now, when he was almost at the end of his quest, it was strange that for the first time since he set out he did not feel as if it mattered whether he found the water to cure his father or not. He felt as if all he wanted to do was to lie down where he was and sleep and sleep and sleep. The trees were asleep, the grass was asleep, even the stones were asleep, and all the people were lying in the fields or even in the roads sleeping as if they would never wake again. Every now and then one of them would mutter something from his dreams, or put out an arm, or stretch his legs, or turn over on his other side with a grunt, but they never woke. Ku-Ling saw two of them get up and unpack rice and begin to cook a meal without ever opening their eyes. Their animals were asleep in the fields beside them, and Ku-Ling longed with all his heart to roll too among the sleeping horses and sheep and people and go to sleep and never

Sleeping as if they would never wake again

wake up again. The air was so soft and heavy it was almost impossible for him to keep his eyes open. Nor did he know how to find the river, for none of the sleeping people would answer him when he asked them.

He might have given up and joined the people of the Country of Sleep for ever, but the good spirits pricked his brain and he managed to force himself to go forward a few steps more, and then he found himself on the banks of a great yellow river, the first he had seen in all his travels. It ran slowly, slowly between its banks, lifting the sleeping weeds and water-lilies and letting them fall again, as if, like Ku-Ling, it was struggling against sleep.

But Ku-Ling took the bottle from his sleeve and filled it with water and as soon as he had done that there was a great rushing through the air and the good spirits who had watched him from the Japonica tree stood before him in the form of great white birds.

They brushed his eyes with their wings and the feeling of sleepiness instantly left him and instead he felt gladder than he had ever felt before in his life.

'You have done well,' said the good spirits, 'many of the people you saw sleeping in the fields came on a similar errand to yours, but none of them endured until they found the river. Now we will spread our wings and you will lie on them and we shall take you home.'

'I promised to give some of this water to the Giant who was kind to me,' said Ku-Ling, 'but I have only one bottle.'

'Dip your scarf in the river and give it to me,' said one of the spirits, 'I will take it to him.'

So Ku-Ling dipped his scarf in the river and gave it

to the good spirit who instantly disappeared with it, and one minute later the scarf wrapped itself round the Giant's middle, and never after that did he feel pain.

Then the good spirit came back, and he and his brother spread their wings, and Ku-Ling lay on them and in one minute he was walking in at the door of his house.

His mother ran to him.

'Oh my son,' she said, 'why did you frighten me by telling me you were going on a long journey, when here you are, back in the house within an hour?'

'To you an hour, to me many days,' said Ku-Ling, taking the bottle of water from the river in the Country of Sleep from his sleeve, 'I have brought what I went to fetch.'

Then he poured a little of the water from the bottle into a cup and took it across to the bed where his father lay, too ill to know who he was or whether he came or went.

At the first sip of water, his father sat up and held out his arms to his son and his wife; at the second sip, he spoke, and at the third sip he sprang out of bed and began to put on his clothes, laughing and rubbing his hands because he was so thankful to be cured. And it was not long before he was back at his work again, making more money than he ever had before, because, although he had always been a clever man and hard working, the water which his good son Ku-Ling brought to him all the way from the Country of Sleep had increased his powers in every way. Soon they went back to their old house with the lattice doors and the gold-fish ponds, and there is not a family in the town who is more honoured than they are.

****
**   **
** Two of Everything **
**   **
****

Two of·Everything

* 🦌 *

MR and Mrs Hak-Tak were rather old and rather
poor. They had a small house in a village among
the mountains and a tiny patch of green land on
the mountain side. Here they grew the vegetables which
were all they had to live on, and when it was a good sea-
son and they did not need to eat up everything as soon as
it was grown, Mr Hak-Tak took what they could spare
in a basket to the next village which was a little larger
than theirs and sold it for as much as he could get and
bought some oil for their lamp, and fresh seeds, and
every now and then, but not often, a piece of cotton
stuff to make new coats and trousers for himself and his
wife. You can imagine they did not often get the chance
to eat meat.

Now, one day it happened that when Mr Hak-Tak was
digging in his precious patch, he unearthed a big brass
pot. He thought it strange that it should have been there
for so long without his having come across it before, and
he was disappointed to find that it was empty; still, he
thought they would find some use for it, so when he was
ready to go back to the house in the evening he decided
to take it with him. It was very big and heavy, and in his
struggles to get his arms round it and raise it to a good
position for carrying, his purse, which he always tock

He unearthed a big brass pot

with him in his belt, fell to the ground, and, to be quite sure he had it safe, he put it inside the pot and so staggered home with his load.

As soon as he got into the house Mrs Hak-Tak hurried from the inner room to meet him.

'My dear husband,' she said, 'whatever have you got there?'

'For a cooking-pot it is too big; for a bath a little too small,' said Mr Hak-Tak. 'I found it buried in our vegetable patch and so far it has been useful in carrying my purse home for me.'

'Alas,' said Mrs Hak-Tak, 'something smaller would have done as well to hold any money we have or are likely to have,' and she stooped over the pot and looked into its dark inside.

As she stooped, her hairpin—for poor Mrs Hak-Tak had only one hairpin for all her hair and it was made of carved bone—fell into the pot. She put in her hand to get it out again, and then she gave a loud cry which brought her husband running to her side.

'What is it?' he asked. 'Is there a viper in the pot?'

'Oh my dear husband,' she cried, 'what can be the meaning of this? I put my hand into the pot to fetch out my hairpin and your purse, and look, I have brought out two hairpins and two purses, both exactly alike.'

'Open the purse. Open both purses,' said Mr Hak-Tak. 'One of them will certainly be empty.'

But not a bit of it. The new purse contained exactly the same number of coins as the old one—for that matter, no one could have said which was the new and which the old—and it meant, of course, that the

Hak-Taks had exactly twice as much money in the evening as they had had in the morning.

'And two hairpins instead of one!' cried Mrs Hak-Tak, forgetting in her excitement to do up her hair which was streaming over her shoulders. 'There is something quite unusual about this pot.'

'Let us put in the sack of lentils and see what happens,' said Mr Hak-Tak, also becoming excited.

They heaved in the bag of lentils and when they pulled it out again—it was so big it almost filled the pot—they saw another bag of exactly the same size waiting to be pulled out in its turn. So now they had two bags of lentils instead of one.

'Put in the blanket,' said Mr Hak-Tak. 'We need another blanket for the cold weather.' And, sure enough, when the blanket came out, there lay another behind it.

'Put my wadded coat in,' said Mr Hak-Tak, 'and then when the cold weather comes there will be one for you as well as for me. Let us put in everything we have in turn. What a pity we have no meat or tobacco, for it seems that the pot cannot make anything without a pattern.'

Then Mrs Hak-Tak, who was a woman of great intelligence, said, 'my dear husband, let us put the purse in again and again and again. If we take two purses out each time we put one in, we shall have enough money by tomorrow evening to buy everything we lack.'

'I am afraid we may lose it this time,' said Mr Hak-Tak, but in the end he agreed, and they dropped in the purse and pulled out two, then they added the new money to the old and dropped it in again and pulled out

the larger amount twice over. After a while the floor was
covered with old leather purses and they decided just to
throw the money in by itself. It worked quite as well
and saved trouble; every time, twice as much money
came out as went in, and every time they added the new
coins to the old and threw them all in together. It took
them some hours to tire of this game, but at last Mrs
Hak-Tak said, 'my dear husband, there is no need for us
to work so hard. We shall see to it that the pot does not
run away, and we can always make more money as we
want it. Let us tie up what we have.'

It made a huge bundle in the extra blanket and the
Hak-Taks lay and looked at it for a long time before
they slept, and talked of all the things they would buy
and the improvements they would make in the cottage.

The next morning they rose early and Mr Hak-Tak
filled a wallet with money from the bundle and set off
for the big village to buy more things in one morning
than he had bought in a whole fifty years.

Mrs Hak-Tak saw him off and then she tidied up the
cottage and put the rice on to boil and had another look
at the bundle of money, and made herself a whole set of
new hairpins from the pot, and about twenty candles instead of the one which was all they had possessed up to
now. After that she slept for a while, having been up so
late the night before, but just before the time when her
husband should be back, she awoke and went over to the
pot. She dropped in a cabbage leaf to make sure it
was still working properly, and when she took two
leaves out she sat down on the floor and put her arms
round it.

'I do not know how you came to us, my dear pot,' she said, 'but you are the best friend we ever had.'

Then she knelt up to look inside it, and at that moment her husband came to the door, and, turning quickly to see all the wonderful things he had bought, she overbalanced and fell into the pot.

Mr Hak-Tak put down his bundles and ran across and caught her by the ankles and pulled her out, but, Oh mercy, no sooner had he set her carefully on the floor than he saw the kicking legs of another Mrs Hak-Tak in the pot! What was he to do? Well, he could not leave her there, so he caught her ankles and pulled, and another Mrs Hak-Tak so exactly like the first that no one would have told one from the other, stood beside them.

'Here's an extraordinary thing,' said Mr Hak-Tak, looking helplessly from one to the other.

'I will not have a second Mrs Hak-Tak in the house!' screamed the old Mrs Hak-Tak.

All was confusion. The old Mrs Hak-Tak shouted and wrung her hands and wept, Mr Hak-Tak was scarcely calmer, and the new Mrs Hak-Tak sat down on the floor as if she knew no more than they did what was to happen next.

'One wife is all *I* want,' said Mr Hak-Tak, 'but how could I have left her in the pot?'

'Put her back in it again!' cried Mrs Hak-Tak.

'What? And draw out two more?' said her husband. 'If two wives are too many for me, what should I do with three? No! No!' He stepped back quickly as if he was stepping away from the three wives and, missing his footing, lo and behold, he fell into the pot!

'*I will not have a second Mrs Hak-Tak in the house!*'

Both Mrs Hak-Taks ran and each caught an ankle and pulled him out and set him on the floor, and there, Oh mercy, was another pair of kicking legs in the pot! Again each caught hold of an ankle and pulled, and soon another Mr Hak-Tak, so exactly like the first that no one could have told one from the other, stood beside them.

Now the old Mr Hak-Tak liked the idea of his double no more than Mrs Hak-Tak had liked the idea of hers. He stormed and raged and scolded his wife for pulling him out of the pot, while the new Mr Hak-Tak sat down on the floor beside the new Mrs Hak-Tak and looked as if, like her, he did not know what was going to happen next.

Then the old Mrs Hak-Tak had a very good idea. 'Listen, my dear husband,' she said, 'now, do stop scolding and listen, for it is really a good thing that there is a new one of you as well as a new one of me. It means that you and I can go on in our usual way, and these new people, who are ourselves and yet not ourselves, can set up house together next door to us.'

And that is what they did. The old Hak-Taks built themselves a fine new house with money from the pot, and they built one just like it next door for the new couple, and they lived together in the greatest friendliness, because as Mrs Hak-Tak said 'The new Mrs Hak-Tak is really more than a sister to me, and the new Mr Hak-Tak is really more than a brother to you.'

The neighbours were very much surprised, both at the sudden wealth of the Hak-Taks and at the new couple who resembled them so strongly that they must, they thought, be very close relations of whom they had never heard before. They said: 'It looks as though the Hak-Taks, when they so unexpectedly became rich, decided to have two of everything, even of themselves, in order to enjoy their money more.'